dreamings of

The
Great Emu War

J. D. YOUNG

Copyright © 2020 J. D. Young

Provincial Publishing

www.provincialpublishing.com.au

All rights reserved.

ISBN: 978-0-6489299-1-8

A catalogue record for this work is available from the National Library of Australia

INSPIRED BY TRUE EVENTS

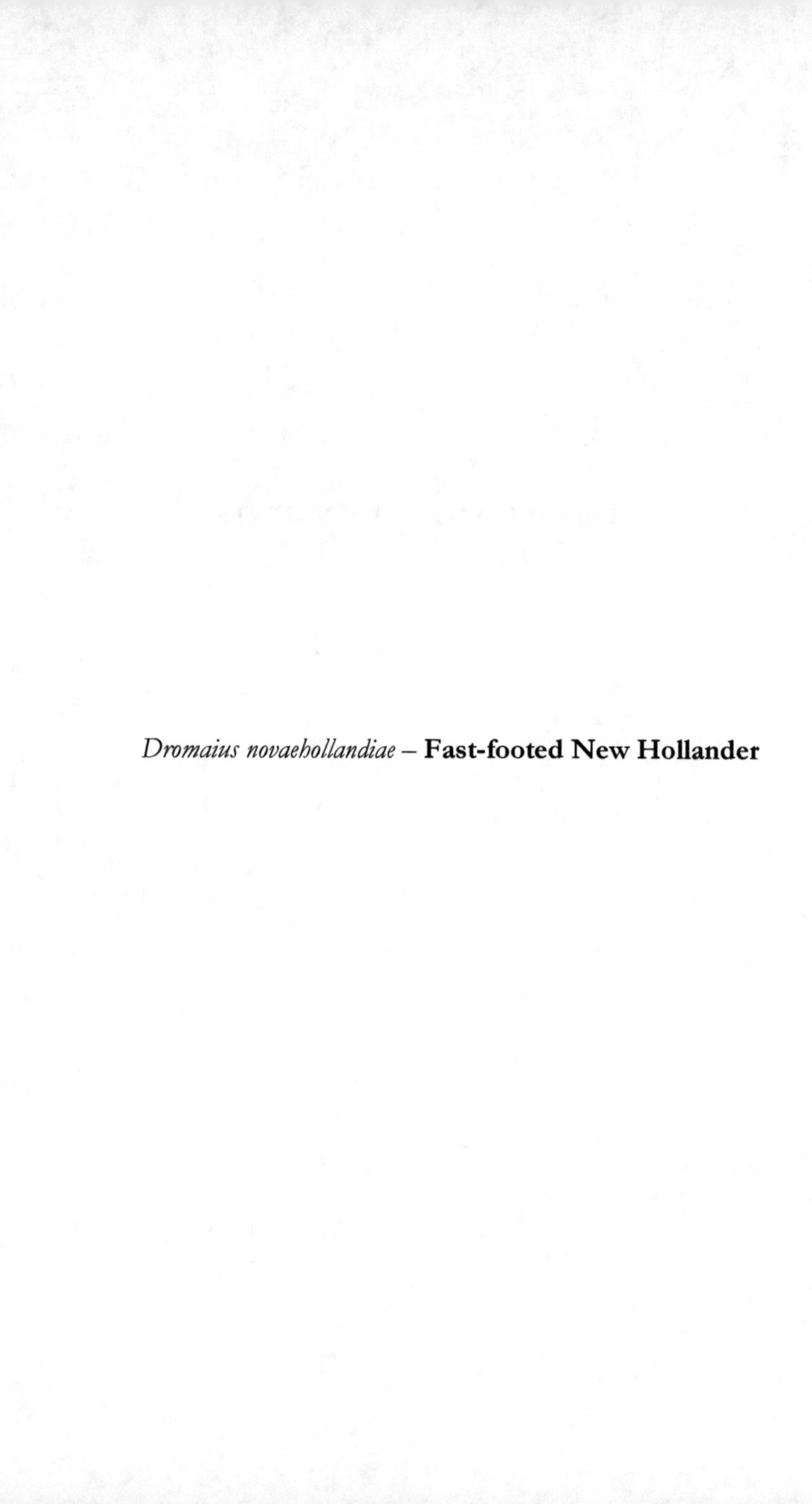

Dromaius novaehollandiae – **Fast-footed New Hollander**

"This is a species differing in many particulars from that generally known, and is a much larger bird, standing higher on its legs and having the neck longer than in the common one. Total length seven feet two inches. The bill is not greatly different from that of the common Cassowary; but the horny appendage, or helmet on top of the head, in this species is totally wanting: the whole of the head and neck is also covered with feathers, except the throat and fore part of the neck about half way, which are not so well feathered as the rest; whereas in the common Cassowary the head and neck are bare and carunculated as in the turkey.

The plumage in general consists of a mixture of brown and grey, and the feathers are somewhat curled or bent at the ends in the natural state: the wings are so very short as to be totally useless for flight, and indeed, are scarcely to be distinguished from the rest of the plumage, were it not for their standing out a little. The long spines which are seen in the wings of the common sort, are in this not observable,— nor is there any appearance of a tail. The legs are stout, formed much as in the Galeated Cassowary, with the addition of their being jagged or sawed the whole of their length at the back part."

- Arthur Philip, *Voyage to Botany Bay*, 1789

1 KAARTDIJIN

1932, Western Australia

The air was getting warmer, the land beneath our feet, dryer. That's how we knew we were in the season of *Kambarang*. It would continue to get hotter and dryer from here onwards, eventually entering into the burning time, the season of *Birak*. But that was yet to come. Today, we and our young families stride proudly across our *boodja*, the land, the country. Picking and foraging and gathering all sorts of deliciousnesses under the warming light of the sun. Wildflowers proliferate the dry landscape at this time of the year. The quandong is one of the most prized treats out here, but its appearance had become rarer in recent seasons, making it all the more sought-after.

We're a nomadic mob, so we don't mind a good walk, or a good run. We go where the opportunities are. For food, for water, for living. Food in this current land was becoming scarce, and with Birak approaching, it was time to continue moving onwards to new land and new opportunities. Endless walking tracks surround us in every direction, across four dimensions. Each brave step puts us at a new shore of this dry ocean. Our options are limitless. The vast landscape looks empty and meaningless, but we know that every place and every thing has its purpose.

We have to take a different route this season, and probably travel further. Kambarang and the lead up to it has been much drier than a typical season. Our wanderings of this season have the goal of heading to the direction of the falling sun. We calculate that this will take us to more food and more water. The populations in that area we also make trade with. We can offer them sought-after *weja*—emu feathers which they use for ornamentation at their ceremonies—of which we have copious supply.

After you travelled through this region, you would eventually reach the edge of the *wardan*, that other oceanic boodja made of salted-water, unpassable, undrinkable, and where the spirits of the dead go to continue their voyage.

But to get where we want to go, we don't follow the sun, not any more than it follows us. We have the unique ability of navigation based on the information given to us by the earth and sky. You see, there is a force generated by the earth which surrounds every place. Detecting and following this force takes us to where we want to go. It appears as a special kind of light, different than that of the sun's.

We are, in truth, champion parents. Father and mother, we are both present to nurture and defend our young with the utmost diligence and care. We teach them the basics like how to find food and water, but also about the nature of life and of the universe. My children are young, and numerous. I teach them the same things with the same methods my parents taught me. We never stop learning and growing, and one can learn as much being a teacher as they can being a student. The more I learn, the more I realise I need to learn.

We teach them all our *kaartdijin*, our knowledge. It's the kaartdijin our parents gave us, and their parents gave them. Our lives, as all things, are eternally cyclical.

One of the earliest things we are taught about is the *Waugal*. The Waugal, who some call the rainbow serpent, is the creator of all things, and giver of life. It provides and maintains all water sources and dominates the earth and sky. Waugal slithered and crafted the long valleys and mountain ranges and lakes into place, at the time of the creation. Waugal created sacred sites, which host both good and bad spirits.

The Waugal still is with us, but usually hidden from sight. It can be disturbed, but you should never disturb the Waugal, it is a dangerous and fearsome entity when disturbed. Deep waterholes and other watery abodes enjoy the Waugal's presence. Always be careful, if you don't treat the Waugal with enough respect, you could lose your fresh water supplies, or your life. If we ever want to swim, we make sure to throw some sand into the water first. This lets the Waugal know of our presence and good intentions.

At the *Nyitting*, the cold time, the ancestral times, the dreamtime, at the very first times of existence of this land, is when the Waugal descended from the sky to create the first landforms and all the first living things. It is from this primordial time that we get our social and moral order, and where we get our knowledge. The Nyitting transcends eternity eternally. It is a transcendental space-time parallel to what you may typically consider time. Everyone exists eternally in this ancestral present, it exists before you and after you. It was the first time, and every other time, existing across everywhen.

The dreamtime kaartdijin is ever-present and interlinked between the boodja and our consciousnesses. The knowledge is in the land and within us too, by virtue of us belonging to the land.

Matter flows from place to place, momentarily coming together to be you. You and I are made of boodja. When you look out at the world, you're looking at yourself.

We learn that *kura*, the past, is always linked with *yey*, the present. Inexorably linked together through space and time. While we, parts of the universe, are not exempt from this principle. Our beings and the universe are inseparable. This realm and the spiritual realm are also connected. All of our ascendants throughout the generations are all an endless continuation. Down to us, and through us into the future. This inter-dimensional web of inter-relationships is where everything in the yey and the kura are connected.

I have thought deeply about these ideas and among my ponderings I have expanded upon them. Imagine an incredible cosmic spider's web on a crisp winter morning, stretching in all directions infinitely, multi-dimensionally, and ultra-dimensionally. Infinite in number, each axis point or dew-drenched jewel of the web contains the reflection of all the other jewels within it. Then, each of the reflections in the jewel contains the reflections of all other dew drops and their reflections, infinitely. Every point contains the information of everything else, and likewise oppositely. This is a way of visually understanding the universe and the interconnectedness of all things. I think of this enchanted web as the *Rainbow Serpent's Web*.

But now as the sun is heading down and the moon

soon ascending, it was time to set up our *koornt*, camp. It is ideal for a camp to be near fresh water, like the *beeliar*, that moving water who tracks around like a long snake. Beeliar were made a long time ago by the Waugal, who created all fresh water. Waugal ensured at creation that there were *wirrin*, or spirits, to look after the land and all that it encompasses.

Our campsite offers lots of nearby fresh water to drink, as well as giving us the opportunity to bathe in the water's cooling refreshment. Water may not be as easy to find after we leave this place. Every night we try to get a good sleep of about seven hours, reinvigorating us for the next daylight.

But when the sky is dark, the lights in the sky gloriously glisten. Just as a tree needs a space to grow up into, the lights in the sky would not be permitted to exist without the darkness around them. There is an inherit quality and absolute necessity about nothingness. Matter and emptiness are inseparable. You cannot have a something, without a nothing, which makes the nothing just as important as the something. As I mentioned earlier, everything has its purpose, even nothing.

When you look into the dark night sky, something very familiar can be seen. Stretched across a vast expanse of the sky is an emu, seemingly leaping across our heads, soaring into the cosmos. But the Emu does not live as the numerous luminous stars, but within the dark patches surrounding these stars. The Celestial Sky Emu shows itself to us not merely for our amusement. Its position tells us when to rest and defend ourselves from external forces, and when it's time to move and explore.

Every night I reach for the starlight all night long, but the pull of the boodja is too strong. Tied to the ground I rest for the moment and think forever just to pass the time.

2 BOKITJA

The earliest moments of a new day begin during the *nanga warloo*, that time when the first new light can be seen, but before the sun itself appears. This is when the first of our mob begin to wake up. Others prefer to continue sleeping until the true daybreak, when the cockatoos begin to sing and squawk.

The early sunlight paints the sky all sorts of sublime colours; fierce slate and lush reds, followed by every hue of blue. Feeling a silky embrace in the morning air, and sun drops dripping refractions in our honey-brown eyes, I feel hungry for the day to start.

While at night we study the stars, in the day we observe the moving sun. I also observe the birds as they fly and soar around. They come in all shapes and sizes and colours and plumages, but all use the sky to travel around with, seemingly effortlessly. I would like to learn how to fly, rather than being tied to the ground, feebly trying to reach for the sky. The fluffy kookaburras love laughing at me while I try to copy their movements, achieving little more than failing miserably. For now, I need to remain content with what I have. At least I can run fast—really fast. So much faster than the kookaburra.

Absorbing the power of the new sun and feeling awakened, our wandering continues onward. We step through truly ancient boodja. It can sometimes seem lonely in this tree-starved vastness, but why should it when we are stepping where countless others have stepped before?

The deep red-brown landscape is scorched and dusty, carpeted by mallee shrublands and boasting few splendid eucalypts. Sources of food were still scarce, but enough to sustain us for now. We take only what we need to ensure that the next time we walk through this boodja, there will be more food for us again.

Many strange and fascinating sites meet us along our

way. There were many sacrosanct caves, some home to great spirits, and some to dark demons. Then there were *gnamma holes*—watering holes. The dry, barren land has water to offer, you just have to know where to look. We know where all the gnamma holes are. We know because our parents taught us, and they know because their parents taught them. The right gnamma holes are always being replenished with new water. Just like how our mob is always on the move in order to survive, water must also move to survive. If water stops moving it slowly begins to rot and become unsuitable for drinking. It is the water that is full of energy and moving and rushing and swimming that is the healthiest water.

We pass many animals, including giddy goannas, cunning dingoes, nifty numbats, and handsome kangaroos. Some give us a glance, but they are mostly indifferent to our presence, as they carry on their business.

There were ancient camping sites and ceremonial grounds. Some have experienced recent use, perhaps being continuously occupied for a very long time. Others, not visited since way back deep into the kura.

Strange formations of giant stones would occasionally greet us. We slalom through bulbous bulbs of sandstone, scree down sloping waves of granite, and find our way around enormous rock walls.

We choose to take a brief respite, and while the others rest, I can't help but be fascinated by my new surroundings. I decide to delicately approach a nearby cave. Slowly dipping my curious head inside and feeling inviting cool air, I gently take a single step inside.

Paintings of dreamscapes adorn the hard stone walls within. Surfaces enigmatically decorated by ancient artists, preserved throughout the ages thanks to shelter offered by the cave against the elements.

Elegant truths and encoded messages from the distant past, locked in place, destined for future eyes to gaze upon. I exit the gallery without taking another step, leaving the haven to hide its secrets.

I learnt last night that some of our mob had heard from another mob of a boodja filled with gold rising high above their heads, where food and water were abundant beyond mere mention. It was said to be in the direction towards the setting sun from here, the direction of the wardan, but not quite as far. This was fortunately the way we were already heading.

We eat the eaten to survive and thrive, but we know that eventually one day the boodja will eat all of us too. When our physical bodies die, they return to the boodja, while our spirits move on to their next destination. Everything in nature tries to eat everything else. Even if we are never eaten by another animal, the land itself will eventually subsume us.

I had a dream last night about the supposed abundant land with towering gold. It was vivid in sight, sensation, and emotion, it felt like I was already there. I certainly recognise it as just a dream, but could dreams be more than just images we imagine in our minds? Deep into a dream and one can experience scenarios as if they were genuine. Sights and sounds and feelings can all be lucidly experienced in a dream, and at times, are indistinguishable to 'reality'. Then is a dream merely a lucubration of our brain, or do we briefly transcend our current existence and pass through a portal into another plane of existence? Why assume one is real and the other false? Just as importantly, what is the difference if they can both be experienced in the same way? Does it matter?

Which leads me to speak about the *Boylyada maaman*. The Boylyada maaman can heal wounds and sicknesses, cause rain to fall, and can even see into the future. We go to him for spiritual wisdom and guidance. Is he able to access parts of this meta-realm at his choosing?

There is then the *kurdaitcha*. Our mob had heard stories of this character from other mobs but had never witnessed him ourselves. He is said to be a sorcerer who performs certain rituals which can cause the death of those the ritual is aimed at. Supposedly, part of the ritual may involve pointing a bone at their target. They also don specially-crafted shoes for the occasion, made from blood and weja, they say. The powers of the Boylyada maaman and Kurdaitcha and the power of dreaming make me know there is more to existence than what we see in our daily life.

In my musings tonight, I wonder how these individuals learn or attain these powers. As a scholar of the stars, I consider it my responsibility to investigate such matters. Everything exists in the dreamtime, the dreamtime is the first time and the eternal everywhen. It could be that if all knowledge and information about the cosmos exists somewhere, that it can be accessed somehow. Those imbued with certain gifts or who have learned these mechanics may be accessing and harnessing this eternal wisdom and using it to their advantage. It must lie within the Rainbow Serpent's Web and understanding its nature, this is how the cosmos is built and so the knowledge of everything must be built into it. This includes all kaartdijin, locked within the Web's records. The right minds tuned to the correct cosmic frequencies can interface with the incredible Web. The Web is full beyond measure of knowledge and truths and the most exquisite interrelationships between everything and everywhen.

3 MERENJ

As we migrated further and further, slowly the dry, sandy ground became firmer, and vegetation became more prolific. In addition to elegant echidnas, wandering wallabies, quaint quolls, and effortlessly suave kangaroos, we walked by unique, docile animals like sheep and cows. Though admiring them from a distance, we could see they were vast in number, all grazing close to one another.

The mob's confidence and excitement grew, knowing that this was the right direction to more bountiful lands. But that is not a disparagement to the lands we have left behind us. Every land has provided for us. We are taught that the dry times are natural, and that dry, barren lands are simply another part of the nature of things. Even though some of us may find them unappealing. The dry, the wet, the cold, the hot, all are necessary.

We relentlessly step over horizon after horizon. As the last horizon falls I see a fantastic glimmer out of the corner of my watering eye. There they were, I could hardly trust my eyes, fields of gold arising out of the barren land. The immense, boundless splendour of the lands of gold struck us like wonder. Just as the other mob had told us about.

Shining brilliantly under the sunlight, the gold showed off nuanced shades and hues across the whole spectrum of golds, trembling gently against a light breeze.

As glorious as the sight is, this gold barely grew to half of our adults' heights, not towering over us as a eucalypt would. Was it the same place? Or had the other mob exaggerated their experience? I didn't care. I stomped into the goldfield as we all did and started eating away at the long pieces of gold that seemed to grow straight out of the ground. I blissfully kicked and fluttered through the field. It was wonderful gold, delicious and stomach-filling.

We all rummaged through the expansive field, eating as much as we could, with the sound of gold rinds cracking violently under our feet as we went along. We met another mob after we had reached the end of the goldfield. They seemed a friendly mob, and told us they knew where more goldfields could be found, so we joined them.

***

In the days that passed, we discovered and consumed more goldfields, and we quenched many thirsts thanks to new sources of fresh water. We picked up a few more mobs along our way. We travelled together, in distinct mobs, but as parts of a greater harmonious whole.

After more walking, we eventually met a strange, impassable object. It was remarkably long, slithering along the ground and into the distance far beyond where we could see. It was decidedly thin, we could easily see through and over it, but it stood too high for us to climb over. Not just too high, but prickly and pointy too. We decided to walk along its length, seeking any way through so that we may pass and continue on our way. Some mobs eventually found, or made their own, cracks in the barrier and got through to the other side.

Although some mobs left us, more joined us, and our total numbers continued to swell. More mobs left us, but even more joined us.

We consumed more gold, we drank more water. The plentiful resources, clear skies, and brilliant sunshine kept us moving together.

Despite our many mobs travelling together, we found a way to coexist productively. Some mobs have mentioned hearing the cries of evil spirits in the distance upon visiting some of the goldfields. So now, each mob has a leader or guard, to keep a watch out for any threats while the mob is in the goldfield.

Over the next days, we too began hearing strange, distant noises. They sounded just like the other mobs described, those of the *warra wirrin*, evil spirits. We also heard the roars of beasts, so loud they must be almighty predators. That's why us mobs need to stay together, to be safe from whatever is out there.

4 BOROONG

The rain delivered by the Waugal has been incessant and astounding. Not seen in more than a long time, the drops of rain have been drenching our bodies and saturating the land for days now. It is still raining, and the rain has caused our grand legion to splinter somewhat. Many of the mobs have scattered. I worry that our fracturing has left us more vulnerable to attacks by the evil spirits.

The dry ground, upon absorbing the rain, has changed. Dust has turned to mud, and already new growths were emerging.

With food and water in supply, and the barrier preventing progress, we think that this might be as far as we need taking our migration. The distant ominous noises we and the other mobs had been hearing have now ceased, maybe driven away by the rains. The rains would eventually stop, but for now we stay safe and the ground stays damp.

I do not know who built the barrier, or why, or how. It may be a natural occurrence, standing since the deep past. It could have been crafted by an idea thought of by a being or animal, but how could they fashion such a grand structure?

It persuades me to contemplate the nature of my own creations and the creations of others, as well as the idea of an idea. I consider when I work a piece of wood to use it in a way to suit my needs, such as to build a bed for my young ones. To say that I, and I alone, have invented or created something would be arrogantly incorrect. I have simply moved and manipulated those which already exist. The wood, the air, the space, all are gifted to me. The idea itself is also not an original of mine, I have just copied what I have seen others do. Original thoughts are impossible, we can just rearrange existing concepts and sift them through our minds to reveal a new concoction of old ideas.

Even when I feel an idea enter my mind, it does not seem like the idea came from me, but rather, to me. Received somewhere from the quintessence, crystallising in my consciousness.

Ideas appear to have life of their own, spreading between host minds, growing and evolving as they go.

If I really wanted to truly invent something from scratch, I would have to create the entire universe itself first.

I didn't even create myself nor my consciousness, rather simply have manifested into this body by powers not mine.

It demonstrates again the inexorable entanglement we all have with the boodja, the cosmos, and the great Rainbow Serpent's Web.

5 FIRST OFFENSIVE

Have you ever had a feeling that you were existing in an experience that was simply *wrong*? I don't just mean that something was not right or not as it should be, but that you or someone or something was cosmically out of place. It's like when you're dreaming and suddenly you escape your subconscious dreaming and lucidly become aware that you're in a dream. Or it's the feeling that you're experiencing a moment again from your past, even though it never happened. Or it's nostalgia for somewhere you've never been to. It's meeting someone you've never met for the second time. It's living within someone else's dream. Like a tear ripping apart the Rainbow Serpent's Web.

This is what remarkably swept over all of us. A presence exploded out of the horizon, beaming with the cacophonous noises of warra wirrin that we thought had finally disappeared. The sensation we felt was as though they had transcended the confines of a dream or a thought and were infiltrating our dimension. This was the attack we prepared for but hoped would never happen.

Horrendous droning and ringing drew closer, it was time to run. Explosive sounds cracked like thunder and lighting, swarming over us like thousands of furious wasps. A showering of sharp, small stones pierced the air with tremendous speed.

Drowning in sound, we all ran, in all different directions to confuse and disorient the belligerents. As I've told you, we are very fast.

We dissipate like mist evaporating off a hot rock. Our scattering and speed would make it hard for the attackers to reach many of us at once.

The projectiles we mostly avoided through our speed and manoeuvrability. Our gangly statures made us harder to pinpoint, and our toughness gave us some immunity from glancing volleys.

The air chokes with plumes of dust risen out from under our feet before the enemy could get close to us.

It was merely moments later that we had outrun them and were safely away and out of their sight.

Our dispersal tactics and immense speed had saved us. A couple of the mob were injured, but nothing a quick consult with the Boylyada maaman wouldn't fix. We regathered and continued on our way.

But what did they want? Had we been accursed by the spirits for wrongdoings? Could they be after revenge? It may reason that the gold belongs to the spirits. It would explain the tremendous bounty of splendour we have been discovering, as it surely eclipses what is possible by the land naturally. It would explain the other-worldly element of what we experienced.

They have declared war, and we won't surrender.

We are hungry.

"The enemy is the tough, prolific, gangling marauder of the sand plains whose species, ever since the beginning of agriculture in the State, has invaded, in a frenzy of hunger, some of the finest fields at the time of ripening of the harvest to shear off crops with voracious beaks and to trample with great webbed feet 100 plants into the earth for each one eaten."

- The Sydney Sunday Herald, 1953

6 BATTLE AT THE DAM

We consolidate the next day, ready for more walking and more eating. We continue with high confidence in our strides despite yesterday's encounter.

After it happened, we consulted with our Boylyada maaman, hoping he would heal us and protect us from the evil spirits. He performed his rituals, to cleanse us of this curse. This would repel the evil, but he could not promise that they would stay away forever. Evil will always exist, just as good will always exist.

The wide plains still surrounded us in what has become a more familiar region. Developing winds whip up from the expanse, drying any residual moisture from my face and body. The radiance of the sun has baked the muddy ground dry and hard. New rain-birthed vegetation sprouts from the ground, sparsely appearing across the brown land.

When we eat, everyone gets to eat, and we all with one another. It brings us together. But even now that we've uncovered the bounty of the goldfields, we are sure not to overindulge. In each field we make sure to not deplete the entire supply, but to leave some behind, so that it has the opportunity to regenerate. Guardians of this country, we consider it our duty to protect it. Not only to ensure we'll have another meal, but because we too are part of the land. If the land is weak, so are we.

During the day, the evil spirits stayed away. The practices of our Boylyada maaman had been effective. In the meantime, more mobs joined and re-joined us. Our clan of collective mobs now increased to numbers vast beyond what I could count. An enormous conglomeration of mobs all travelling with determination. I felt confident that if the evil spirits were able to somehow reach and attack us again, that at least our formidable strength in numbers would scare them off.

Still disheveled and thirsty after relentless walking and running, we seek out water. We tracked towards known gnamma holes. In this deep heat and pounding sunlight, fresh water would replenish our thirsts and hearts so well.

***

During the next day of walking we unexpectedly notice large portions of water in the distance. It was a gnamma hole none of us had known about. Drawing ever closer, myself and some others had taken guard positions, to keep watch in case of impending trouble. Water is a precious and important resource, after all.

After the others had finished taking their turns drinking, I earn my opportunity to rehydrate and I gulp the water down like a cold beverage. Fallen grevilleas lay in the water, infusing it with a touch of floral sweetness.

Before I could down my next and final gulp, our refreshments were interrupted again by a striking tension.

That same existential discomfort of two days prior

was felt by us all. The second apparition of those evil ultra-terrestrial, pan-dimensional, fire-spitting spirits. I raised the alarm as soon as I could, and instantly we all began to strategically scatter.

Charging through the battlefield, shrieks ring out with a tremendous sound, and the air around us is ripped into pieces. This attack feels more intense than the last. The spirits were closer, attacked with more firepower. Searingly hot embers sting us with the poison of ten thousand scorpion tails.

As we were running, I saw a couple in the mob stop in their tracks, legs collapsing under their bodies. Succumbed to the evil spirits. But I had to keep running. I urged our stampede to keep moving.

Two leaps further and I feel a blistering blow, my legs give way and I crash to the hard ground below. Poisoned by the spirits' missile. Suffering an utterly awful agony, my body tumbles along the rough ground, picking up dust and sand, as my speed comes to a stop.

7 BARDAN-KOORL

I awoke from a deep sleep to find myself in pain and covered in dust. I could barely open my eyes, my eyelids heavy and stinging with sand.

Slowly I lift myself out from the sand drifts eager to envelop me, one body part at a time, eventually making it to my two feet. It was difficult to make out my surroundings with these irritated dry eyes. But I already knew that I was alone.

I know that despite my solitude and injuries, I had been lucky. Memories of besiegement and torment and crashing are haunting to recall.

Among the chaotic scenes, it's likely I witnessed lives of ones I know be taken from this world. Their spirits already well into their new journey.

As sand crunches in my mouth, I shake off the remaining dust from my body, and I know what I must do next. I have to keep walking. My pace will be greatly slowed, but I can still sense enough from my surroundings to know which direction to go.

I'm bound to rejoin my mob at some point. They're out there somewhere across the flat, weathered ground, beyond the horizon.

There is an ancient labyrinth of tracks meandering across the land and sky. But you need to know how to identity and access these routes. It can be difficult. Much as how the wardan has tides, so does the desert. You need to use more than what you can just touch and see. My mob would have used the same tracks, so I'm bound to reunite with them once our paths inevitably meet.

That's if there's still a mob to find.

I've got a lot of lone walking to do, which means I have the chance to do a lot of thinking. There's something about the solitude and repetition of walking that I find conducive to deep thinking.

While I was knocked unconscious, the evil spirits had a chance to kill me, yet I'm still alive. Did something protect me? If we ever meet again, will they remember me?

With life and death, I always think again of contrasts and the notion of something versus nothing. We are expressions of the universe, we are a way which allows it to think and contemplate its existence. If you didn't have a consciousness it would be impossible to imagine what it would be like to have one. The only reason we know we're alive is because we used to be not alive.

Will we then in post-life, after having experienced being alive, be able to fathom what it is we are experiencing, as opposed to pre-life where we had no point of reference?

Each step hurts, but I keep walking along a track I know. Onwards through the dust and shrubs and grasses for as long as I have to.

We are strong as a mob, but I'm vulnerable on my own. If the spirits don't get me, maybe the land will. But I'll struggle and I'll overcome, before the desert subdues me to my rusty knees. The boodja is with me. I need the mob and the mob needs me.

A long day of painful walking was about to be put to rest by another sunset. The Celestial Sky Emu begins to reveal itself, soaring passionately through the heavens high above me. It's a calming and reassuring presence. I would usually set up camp and prepare to sleep by nightfall, but not tonight. I ride onwards through the black air. Without the sun, cold quickly bites into the darkness.

Carrying on with determination, the stars and moon glow vibrantly overhead. Yet I spot another distinct set of lights flicker along a point just above the horizon. These spheres of light begin to radiate and move about on their own volition. There's something mighty eerie in these dazzling dancing lights.

My walking becomes running and my focus becomes scattered. I melt as I'm bathed in the chill of the moonlight.

I didn't even notice that I've been wrenched from the track I was following and now I'm waywardly rampaging towards the moving lights. I should be retreating to safety but I'm drawn to these balls of light, now radiating from white to red and back again.

I've been running for some time now, but the lights aren't getting any closer. It feels like I can almost touch them, yet they look so far away. Are they moving further away from me as I draw nearer? Are my eyes trying to show me glimmers of false hope? Am I still recovering from my injuries?

I want to meet you, dear sublime satellites. There's so many things I have to tell you of. Please don't leave.

The lights still seem as distant as ever, yet I'm closing into a presence. It's erratic and violent.

I keep running and I'm fearful but my mind races faster than my legs do. How do I know I am who I think I am, and who is the real me?

I'm still badly injured but sensations of pain have disappeared.

The bizarre lights and the Celestial Sky Emu appear almost in tandem in the sky. Their astral dance fluxes and flows with superb grace. Could the lights be messages, or messengers, from the great Emu?

It feels like there's a skirmish up ahead. It's still distant but I see dust pluming high.

I should have stayed on my own track, but the lure of the lights is impacting me viscerally. What are they trying to tell me?

The lights still move about, they want me to catch them, but I can't. They continue to lure me, taunting me, but there's a beaming of salvation in these lights that I can't resist.

My desperation ends when I happen across the skirmish. I run into engulfing plumes of dust and I'm blind.

I run to the peak of a ridge and I scree to a stop, my feet fueling the plumes. I still feel an energy, but as the dust settles, there's no melee, brawl, or skirmish in sight.

Instead, I see a rather tame and unremarkable camp. It's my mob, sleeping as they should be. Without me, as they shouldn't be.

8 WAITCHERUP

They assure me we were now in safety, so I begin to tell the mob my story. My heart rate gradually slows down, and as it does, my pain returns.

As I was explaining what happened, the Boylyada maaman came to me and looked at my injuries. He removed the spirits' poison, treated me with his medicinal powder, and removed the impurities I had become inflicted with.

To my surprise, the mob gives a nonchalant reaction to my recount. Apparently, they'd had a similar experience to mine. Mesmerised by those tempting, menacing balls of light, beckoning them to this place. I want to know more but I want to know more about something else even more. I need to know what happened during our last battle at the watering hole, where I was taken down.

It could have been worse. Incredibly, despite the evil spirits' almighty armaments and incredible power, our manoeuvres and speed had once again protected us, mostly.

Heartbreakingly, a bunch of the mob were missing. No doubt devoured by the spirits. It took an emotional pain on our families. Our fallen ones we mourn deeply, even those of the other mobs. Our kinship and empathy extends beyond our own mob, reaching other mobs too. It would lay heavy in our minds for some time to come. It was the price we paid for what we had received.

Recovering, I had the chance to reflect on the attack and our losses. To contemplate its significance and meaning. How were we able to escape relatively easily, despite the spirits' immense power? Did they give up? Why? Or perhaps efforts of our Boylyada maaman were successful. Or simply, maybe we really are too fast and cunning.

I asked the Boylyada maaman what the bizarre balls of light could have been and what could be the significance of this event. He finished up his treatments on me and began to attempt an explanation.

He tells me the lights could be spirit ancestors. They heeded the call of his rituals and came to save us from the evil that was attacking us. Proffering help when we needed it the most.

We mourn our losses and scorn the evil spirits, but what if they too are just trying to survive and protect what they have, just as we do? They have the right to defend what they believe is theirs. We did not create or earn this gold, we merely happened across it. But we also must respect and defend ourselves. Are these attacks of desperation? Cries for help? Can I free them from their curse, or are they the curse? Can I save them before they force the entire sky, along with the Sky Emu, down upon us?

Looking up, the Sky Emu bravely maintains a fearless disposition, and gestures that we keep moving onwards. I told you, this is war. We are still thirsty, we are still hungry.

"If we had a military division with the bullet-carrying capacity of these birds it would face any army in the world. They can face machine guns with the invulnerability of tanks."

- Major G. P. W. Meredith, Royal Australian Artillery

9 CRESTFALLEN FORCE

Over the next few days that passed, the evil spirits again returned and continued to follow and harass us. They were after war, and our blood.

Their appearance was always accompanied by the same dread and the same noise. Myself and the guards of other mobs are now needed to not just serve as security, but as soldiers. They attacked us again and again, each time we outran and outmanoeuvred them. We managed to escape with only a few injuries after each attack.

There was finally a day without incident. We think the enemy has surrendered, but I know it was only going to be temporary. The war between good and evil is eternal.

This sounds like an unpleasant state to be in, but it is a natural quality of being and of the cosmos. Good would not be permitted to exist at all without bad. Evil tries to tear me down, to destroy and corrupt. Yet I do not seek to dominate, only to empower.

Part of life, we constantly have the urge to fight against evil, it's etched into our ancient soul memory. Evil will never disappear completely, but we can do our best to live our best.

We travel far distances to discover food and water, but more than our physical journeys, we go through mental and spiritual journeys to grow, adapt, learn. Turmoil that at first felt like a taste of poison to my spirit has forced my maturity to accelerate and my wisdom to grow with the fragrance of nectar. Duty, responsibility, and practice bring serenity and happiness. The ruin of reason leads to destruction.

I already need to plan how to avoid the perils we faced this season the next time we migrate through here. It could have been much worse, and next season, the warra wirrin might devise new tactics to destroy us.

I cannot say for certainty what may happen in the

future, but I retain a burning wistfulness for the future. All I can say is that evil and good will always continue to exist.

This is not to say that we are the ultimate archetype of 'good'. We are not perfect. What if the spirits we call 'evil' are the good ones, and we the evil? Does evil know that it is evil? From another perspective, we have destroyed their homes, eaten all their food, and now they are starving.

The days continue, we keep finding more goldfields to consume, and more new gnamma holes to consume. We keep sensing and hearing the spirits in the distance, but never again with unfortunate incident.

They knew we were here, they knew we were still taking their gold, but stopped their attacks. Likely deterred by the will of our ancestor spirits.

More days pass, we eat more, we remain safe. Our defence campaign has been successful, if with some extra help, and the gold belongs to use once more. We consider ourselves victors in this war.

But as they are ever-present, we know they would

return. We must always keep our instincts alert and our defences vigilant. But for now, we are confident that the gold is ours. Our boodja is ours.

We have had plenty of food and water, the goldfields have provided for us more than expected. As always, we restrain ourselves and never consume to exhaustion. The gold will grow again.

The fiery Birak season was commencing, and we are moving on. But we're always on the move, we're a nomadic mob after all, and we will return to this place again another season.

We all adore that feeling of love and togetherness. But it seems with that happiness always comes a tiny element of sadness. It's because inside, we know the transience of life. Nothing will ever stay as it does now forever.

But is time really destroyed as it passes? Or maybe we're just walking through a boulevard of time, taking a glance at each pebble in the road, as we continue to the next step. The road still exists, we're just further down it.

As hard as it is to lose something, it feels perhaps

harder and gives me more fear to lose something I've never had. An unquenchable nostalgia for what has never happened.

I'm a light sleeper, but I'm a heavy dreamer.

"The machine-gunners' dreams of point blank fire into serried masses of Emus were soon dissipated. The Emu command had evidently ordered guerrilla tactics, and its unwieldy army soon split up into innumerable small units that made use of the military equipment uneconomic. A crestfallen field force therefore withdrew from the combat area after about a month."

-    Dominic Serventy, ornithologist

ACKNOWLEDGEMENTS

This text features words from the Noongar language, indigenous to south-western Western Australia. It consists of over a dozen dialects, and because it is an oral language, there are many variations in usage and spelling. Spelling used in this text should not be taken as definitive, only as one variation.

Language heritage and knowledge of words and themes remains with the Traditional Owners and language custodians.

Although inspired by actual events, any characters in this text are fictional and no real persons are implied. Nothing should be taken as representative of anyone.